LOVE AMONG
THE HAYSTACKS

D. H. LAWRENCE

LOVE AMONG
THE HAYSTACKS

penguin books

PENGUIN BOOKS

Published by the Penguin Group
Penguin Books USA Inc., 375 Hudson Street,
New York, New York 10014, U.S.A.
Penguin Books Ltd, 27 Wrights Lane,
London W8 5TZ, England
Penguin Books Australia Ltd, Ringwood,
Victoria, Australia
Penguin Books Canada Ltd, 10 Alcorn Avenue,
Toronto, Ontario, Canada M4V 3B2
Penguin Books (N.Z.) Ltd, 182–190 Wairau Road,
Auckland 10, New Zealand

Penguin Books Ltd, Registered Offices:
Harmondsworth, Middlesex, England

Published in Penguin Books 1995

ISBN 0 14 60.0091 9

Printed in the United States of America

The two large fields lay on a hillside facing south. Being newly cleared of hay, they were golden green, and they shone almost blindingly in the sunlight. Across the hill, half-way up, ran a high hedge, that flung its black shadow finely across the molten glow of the sward. The stack was being built just above the hedge. It was of great size, massive, but so silvery and delicately bright in tone that it seemed not to have weight. It rose dishevelled and radiant among the steady, golden-green glare of the field. A little farther back was another, finished stack.

The empty wagon was just passing through the gap in the hedge. From the far-off corner of the bottom field, where the sward was still striped grey with winrows, the loaded wagon launched forward to climb the hill to the stack. The white dots of the hay-makers showed distinctly among the hay.

The two brothers were having a moment's rest, waiting for the load to come up. They stood wiping their brows with their arms, sighing from the heat and the labour of placing the last load. The stack they rode was high, lifting them up above the hedge-tops, and very broad, a great slightly-hollowed vessel into which the sunlight poured, in which the hot, sweet scent of hay was suffocating. Small and inefficacious the brothers looked, half-submerged in the loose, great trough, lifted high up as if on an altar reared to the sun.

Maurice, the younger brother, was a handsome young fellow of twenty-one, careless and debonair, and full of vigour. His grey eyes, as he taunted his brother, were bright and baffled with a strong emotion. His swarthy face had the same peculiar smile, expectant and glad and nervous, of a young man roused for the first time in passion.

"Tha sees," he said, as he leaned on the pommel of his fork "tha thowt as tha'd done me one, didna ter?" He smiled as he spoke, then fell again into his pleasant torment of musing.

"I thought nowt—tha knows so much," retorted Geoffrey, with the touch of a sneer. His brother had the better of him. Geoffrey was a very heavy, hulking fellow, a year older than Maurice. His blue eyes were unsteady, they glanced away quickly; his mouth was morbidly sensitive. One felt him wince away, through the whole of his great body. His inflamed self-consciousness was a disease in him.

"Ah, but though, I know tha did," mocked Maurice. "Tha went slinkin' off"—Geoffrey winced convulsively— "thinking as that wor the last night as any of us'ud ha'e ter stop here, an' so tha'd leave me to sleep out, though it wor they turn——"

He smiled to himself, thinking of the result of Geoffrey's ruse.

"I didna go slinkin' off neither," retorted Geoffrey, in his heavy, clumsy manner, wincing at the phrase. "Didna my feyther send me to fetch some coal——"

"Oh yes, oh yes—we know all about it. But tha sees what tha missed, my lad."

Maurice, chuckling, threw himself on his back in the bed of hay. There was absolutely nothing in his world, then, except the shallow ramparts of the stack, and the blazing sky. He clenched his fists tight, threw his arms across his face, and braced his muscles again. He was evidently very much moved, so acutely that it was hardly pleasant, though he still smiled. Geoffrey, standing behind him, could just see his red mouth, with the young moustache like black fur, curling back and showing the teeth in a smile. The elder brother leaned his chin on the pommel of his fork, looking out across the country.

Far away was the faint blue heap of Nottingham. Between, the country lay under a haze of heat, with here and there a flag of colliery smoke waving. But near at hand, at the foot of the hill, across the deep-hedged high road, was only the silence of the old church and the castle farm, among their trees. The large view only made Geoffrey more sick. He looked away, to the wagons crossing the field below him, the empty cart like a big insect moving down-hill, the load coming up, rocking like a ship, the brown head of the horse ducking, the brown knees lifted and planted strenuously. Geoffrey wished it would be quick.

"Tha didna think——"

Geoffrey started, coiled within himself, and looked down at the handsome lips moving in speech below the brown arms of his brother.

"Tha didna think 'er'd be thur wi' me—or tha wouldna ha' left me to it," Maurice said, ending with a little laugh of excited memory. Geoffrey flushed with hate, and had an impulse to set his foot on that moving, taunting mouth, which was there below him. There was silence for a time, then, in a peculiar tone of delight, Maurice's voice came again, spelling out the words as it were:

> *"Ich bin klein, mein Herz ist rein,*
> *Ist niemand d'rin als Christ allein."*

Maurice chuckled, then, convulsed at a twinge of recollection, keen as pain, he twisted over, pressed himself into the hay.

"Can thee say thy prayers in German?" came his muffled voice.

"I non want," growled Geoffrey.

Maurice chuckled. His face was quite hidden, and in

the dark he was going over again his last night's experiences.

"What about kissing 'er under th' ear, Sonny," he said, in a curious, uneasy tone. He writhed, still startled and inflamed by his first contact with love.

Geoffrey's heart swelled within him, and things went dark. He could not see the landscape.

"An' there's just a nice two-handful of her bosom," came the low, provocative tones of Maurice, who seemed to be talking to himself.

The two brothers were both fiercely shy of women, and until this hay harvest, the whole feminine sex had been represented by their mother and in presence of any other women they were dumb louts. Moreover, brought up by a proud mother, a stranger in the country, they held the common girls as beneath them, because beneath their mother, who spoke pure English, and was very quiet. Loud-mouthed and broad-tongued the common girls were. So these two young men had grown up virgin but tormented.

Now again Maurice had the start of Geoffrey, and the elder brother was deeply mortified. There was a danger of his sinking into a morbid state, from sheer lack of living, lack of interest. The foreign governess at the Vicarage, whose garden lay beside the top field, had talked to the lads through the hedge, and had fascinated them. There was a great elder bush, with its broad creamy flowers 5 crumbling on to the garden path, and into the field. Geoffrey never smelled elder-flower without starting and wincing, thinking of the strange foreign voice that had so startled him as he mowed out with the scythe in the hedge bottom. A baby had run through the gap, and the Fräulein, calling in German, had come brushing down the flowers in pursuit. She had started so on seeing a man standing there in the shade, that for a moment she could not move: and then she had blundered into the rake which was lying by his side. Geoffrey, forgetting she was a woman when he saw her pitch forward, had picked her up carefully, asking: "Have you hurt you?"

Then she had broken into a laugh, and answered in German, showing him her arms, and knitting her brows. She was nettled rather badly.

"You want a dock leaf," he said. She frowned in a puzzled fashion.

"A dock leaf?" she repeated. He had rubbed her arms with the green leaf.

And now, she had taken to Maurice. She had seemed to prefer himself at first. Now she had sat with Maurice in the moonlight, and had let him kiss her. Geoffrey sullenly suffered, making no fight.

Unconsciously, he was looking at the Vicarage garden. There she was, in a golden-brown dress. He took off his hat, and held up his right hand in greeting to her. She, a 6 small, golden figure, waved her hand negligently from among the potato rows. He remained, arrested, in the same posture, his hat in his left hand, his right arm upraised, thinking. He could tell by the negligence of her greeting that she was waiting for Maurice. What did she think of himself? Why wouldn't she have him?

Hearing the voice of the wagoner leading the load, Maurice rose. Geoffrey still stood in the same way, but his face was sullen, and his upraised hand was slack with brooding. Maurice faced up-hill. His eyes lit up and he laughed. Geoffrey dropped his own arm, watching.

"Lad!" chuckled Maurice. "I non knowed 'er wor there." He waved his hand clumsily. In these matters Geoffrey did better. The elder brother watched the girl. She ran to the end of the path, behind the bushes, so that she was screened from the house. Then she waved her handkerchief wildly. Maurice did not notice the manœuvre. There was the cry of a child. The girl's figure vanished, reappeared holding up a white childish bundle, and came down the path. There she put down her charge, sped up-hill to a great ash tree, climbed quickly to a large horizontal bar that formed the fence there, and, standing poised, blew kisses with both her hands, in a foreign fashion that excited the brothers. Maurice laughed aloud, as he waved his red handkerchief.

"Well, what's the danger?" shouted a mocking voice from below. Maurice collapsed, blushing furiously.

"Nowt!" he called.

There was a hearty laugh from below.

The load rode up, sheered with a hiss against the stack, then sank back again upon the scotches. The brothers ploughed across the mass of hay, taking the forks. Presently a big burly man, red and glistening, climbed to the top of the load. Then he turned round, scrutinised the hillside from under his shaggy brows. He caught sight of the girl under the ash tree.

"Oh, that's who it is," he laughed. "I thought it was some such bird, but I couldn't see her."

The father laughed in a hearty, chaffing way, then began to teem the load. Geoffrey, on the stack above, received his great forkfuls, and swung them over to Maurice, who took them, placed them, building the stack. In the intense sunlight, the three worked in silence, knit together in a brief passion of work. The father stirred slowly for a moment, getting the hay from under his feet. Geoffrey waited, the blue tines of his fork glittering in expectation: the mass rose, his fork swung beneath it, there was a light clash of blades, then the hay was swept on to the stack, caught by Maurice, who placed it judiciously. One after another, the shoulders of the three men bowed and braced themselves. All wore light blue, bleached shirts, that stuck close to their backs. The father moved mechanically, his thick, rounded shoulders bending and lifting dully: he worked monotonously. Geoffrey flung away his strength. His massive shoulders swept and flung the hay extravagantly.

"Dost want to knock me ower?" asked Maurice angrily. He had to brace himself against the impact. The three men worked intensely, as if some will urged them. Maurice was light and swift at the work, but he had to use his judgment. Also, when he had to place the hay along the far ends, he had some distance to carry it. So he was too slow for Geoffrey. Ordinarily, the elder would have placed the hay as far as possible where his brother wanted it. Now, however, he pitched his forkfuls into the middle of the stack. Maurice strode swiftly and handsomely across the bed, but the work was too much for him. The other two men, clinched in their receive and deliver, kept up a high pitch of labour. Geoffrey still flung the hay at random. Maurice was perspiring heavily with heat and exertion, and was getting worried. Now and again, Geoffrey wiped his arm across his brow, mechanically, like an animal. Then he glanced with satisfaction at Maurice's moiled condition, and caught the next forkful.

"Wheer dost think thou'rt hollin' it, fool!" panted Maurice, as his brother flung a forkful out of reach.

"Wheer I've a mind," answered Geoffrey.

Maurice toiled on, now very angry. He felt the sweat trickling down his body: drops fell into his long black lashes, blinding him, so that he had to stop and angrily dash his eyes clear. The veins stood out in his swarthy neck. He felt he would burst, or drop, if the work did not soon slacken off. He heard his father's fork dully scrape the cart bottom.

"There, the last," the father panted. Geoffrey tossed the last light lot at random, took off his hat, and, steaming in the sunshine as he wiped himself, stood complacently watching Maurice struggle with clearing the bed.

"Don't you think you've got your bottom corner a bit far out?" came the father's voice from below. "You'd better be drawing in now, hadn't you?"

"I though you said next load," Maurice called sulkily.

"Aye. All right. But isn't this bottom corner——?"

Maurice, impatient, took no notice.

Geoffrey strode over the stack, and stuck his fork in the offending corner. "What—here?" he bawled in his great voice.

"Aye—isn't it a bit loose?" came the irritating voice.

Geoffrey pushed his fork in the jutting corner, and, leaning his weight on the handle, shoved. He thought it shook. He thrust again with all his power. The mass swayed.

"What art up to, tha fool!" cried Maurice, in a high voice.

"Mind who tha'rt callin' a fool," said Geoffrey, and he prepared to push again. Maurice sprang across, and elbowed his brother aside. On the yielding, swaying bed of hay, Geoffrey lost his foothold and fell grovelling. Maurice tried the corner.

"It's solid enough," he shouted angrily.

"Aye—all right," came the conciliatory voice of the father; "you do get a bit of rest now there's such a long way to cart it," he added reflectively.

Geoffrey had got to his feet.

"Tha'll mind who tha'rt nudging, I can tell thee," he threatened heavily; adding, as Maurice continued to work, "an' tha non ca's him a fool again, dost hear?"

"Not till next time," sneered Maurice.

As he worked silently round the stack, he neared where his brother stood like a sullen statue, leaning on his forkhandle, looking out over the countryside. Maurice's heart quickened in its beat. He worked forward, until a point of his fork caught in the leather of Geoffrey's boot, and the metal rang sharply.

"Are ter going ta shift thysen?" asked Maurice threateningly. There was no reply from the great block. Maurice lifted his upper lip like a dog. Then he put out his elbow and tried to push his brother into the stack, clear of his way.

"Who are ter shovin'?" came the deep, dangerous voice. "Thaïgh," replied Maurice, with a sneer, and straightway the two brothers set themselves against each other, like opposing bulls, Maurice trying his hardest to shift Geoffrey from his footing, Geoffrey leaning all his weight 11 in resistance. Maurice, insecure in his footing, staggered a little, and Geoffrey's weight followed him. He went slithering over the edge of the stack.

Geoffrey turned white to the lips, and remained standing, listening. He heard the fall. Then a flush of darkness came over him, and he remained standing only because he was planted. He had not strength to move. He could hear no sound from below, was only faintly aware of a sharp shriek from a long way off. He listened again. Then he filled with sudden panic.

"Feyther!" he roared, in his tremendous voice: "Feyther! Feyther!"

The valley re-echoed with the sound. Small cattle on the hillside looked up. Men's figures came running from the bottom field, and much nearer a woman's figure was racing across the field. Geoffrey waited in terrible suspense.

"Ah-h!" he heard the strange, wild voice of the girl cry out. "Ah-h!"—and then some foreign wailing speech. Then: "Ah-h! Are you dea-ed!"

He stood sullenly erect on the stack, not daring to go down, longing to hide in the hay, but too sullen to stoop out of sight. He heard his eldest brother come up, panting:

"Whatever's amiss!" and then the labourer, and then his father.

"Whatever have you been doing?" he heard his father

ask, while yet he had not come round the corner of the stack. And then, in a low, bitter tone:

"Eh, he's done for! I'd no business to ha' put it all on that stack."

There was a moment or two of silence, then the voice of Henry, the eldest brother, said crisply:

"He's not dead—he's coming round."

Geoffrey heard, but was not glad. He had as lief Maurice were dead. At least that would be final: better than meeting his brother's charges, and of seeing his mother pass to the sick-room. If Maurice was killed, he himself would not explain, no, not a word, and they could hang him if they liked. If Maurice were only hurt, then everybody would know, and Geoffrey could never lift his face again. What added torture, to pass along, everybody knowing. He wanted something that he could stand back to, something definite, if it were only the knowledge that he had killed his brother. He *must* have something firm to back up to, or he would go mad. He was so lonely, he who above all needed the support of sympathy.

"No, he's commin' to; I tell you he is," said the labourer.

"He's not dea-ed, he's not dea-ed," came the passionate, strange sing-song of the foreign girl. "He's not dead—no-o."

"He wants some brandy—look at the colour of his

lips," said the crisp, cold voice of Henry. "Can you fetch some?"

"Wha-at? Fetch?" Fräulein did not understand.

"Brandy," said Henry, very distinct.

"Brrandy!" she re-echoed.

"You go, Bill," groaned the father.

"Aye, I'll go," replied Bill, and he ran across the field.

Maurice was not dead, nor going to die. This Geoffrey now realised. He was glad after all that the extreme penalty was revoked. But he hated to think of himself going on. He would always shrink now. He had hoped and hoped for the time when he would be careless, bold as Maurice, when he would not wince and shrink. Now he would always be the same, coiling up in himself like a tortoise with no shell.

"Ah-h! He's getting better!" came the wild voice of the Fräulein, and she began to cry, a strange sound, that startled the men, made the animal bristle within them. Geoffrey shuddered as he heard, between her sobbing, the impatient moaning of his brother as the breath came back.

The labourer returned at a run, followed by the Vicar. After the brandy, Maurice made more moaning, hiccuping noise. Geoffrey listened in torture. He heard the Vicar asking for explanations. All the united, anxious voices replied in brief phrases.

"It was that other," cried the Fräulein. "He knocked him over—Ha!"

She was shrill and vindictive.

"I don't think so," said the father to the Vicar, in a quite audible but private tone, speaking as if the Fräulein did not understand his English.

The Vicar addressed his children's governess in bad German. She replied in a torrent which he would not confess was too much for him. Maurice was making little moaning, sighing noises.

"Where's your pain, boy, eh?" the father asked pathetically.

"Leave him alone a bit," came the cool voice of Henry. "He's winded, if no more."

"You'd better see that no bones are broken," said the anxious Vicar.

"It wor a blessing as he should a dropped on that heap of hay just there," said the labourer. "If he'd happened to ha' catched hisself on this nog o' wood 'e wouldna ha' stood much chance."

Geoffrey wondered when he would have courage to venture down. He had wild notions of pitching himself head foremost from the stack: if he could only extinguish himself, he would be safe. Quite frantically, he longed not to be. The idea of going through life thus coiled up within himself in morbid self-consciousness, always lonely, surly, and a misery, was enough to make him cry out. What would they all think when they knew he had knocked Maurice off that high stack?

They were talking to Maurice down below. The lad had recovered in great measure, and was able to answer faintly.

"Whatever was you doin'?" the father asked gently. "Was you playing about with our Geoffrey?—Aye, and where is he?"

Geoffrey's heart stood still.

"I dunno," said Henry, in a curious, ironic tone.

"Go an' have a look," pleaded the father, infinitely relieved over one son, anxious now concerning the other. Geoffrey could not bear that his eldest brother should climb up and question him in his high-pitched drawl of curiosity. The culprit doggedly set his feet on the ladder. His nailed boots slipped a rung.

"Mind yourself," shouted the over-wrought father.

Geoffrey stood like a criminal at the foot of the ladder, glancing furtively at the group. Maurice was lying, pale and slightly convulsed, upon a heap of hay. The Fräulein was kneeling beside his head. The Vicar had the lad's shirt full open down the breast, and was feeling for broken ribs. The father kneeled on the other side, the labourer and Henry stood aside.

"I can't find anything broken," said the Vicar, and he sounded slightly disappointed.

"There's nowt broken to find," murmured Maurice, smiling.

The father started. "Eh?" he said. "Eh?" and he bent
16 over the invalid.

"I say it's not hurt me," repeated Maurice.

"What were you doing?" asked the cold, ironic voice of Henry. Geoffrey turned his head away: he had not yet raised his face.

"Nowt as I know on," he muttered in a surly tone.

"Why!" cried Fräulein in a reproachful tone. "I see him—knock him over!" She made a fierce gesture with her elbow. Henry curled his long moustache sardonically.

"Nay lass, niver," smiled the wan Maurice. "He was fur enough away from me when I slipped."

"Oh, ah!" cried the Fräulein, not understanding.

"Yi," smiled Maurice indulgently.

"I think you're mistaken," said the father, rather pathetically, smiling at the girl as if she were 'wanting.'

"Oh no," she cried. "I *see* him."

"Nay, lass," smiled Maurice quietly.

She was a Pole, named Paula Jablonowsky: young, only twenty years old, swift and light as a wild cat, with a strange, wild-cat way of grinning. He hair was blonde and full of life, all crisped into many tendrils with vitality, shaking round her face. Her fine blue eyes were peculiarly lidded, and she seemed to look piercingly, then languorously, like a wild cat. She had somewhat Slavonic cheekbones, and was very much freckled. It was evident that the Vicar, a pale, rather cold man, hated her.

Maurice lay pale and smiling in her lap, whilst she cleaved to him like a mate. One felt instinctively that 17 they were mated. She was ready at any minute to fight with ferocity in his defence, now he was hurt. Her looks at Geoffrey were full of fierceness. She bowed over Maurice and caressed him with her foreign-sounding English.

"You say what you lai-ike," she laughed, giving him lordship over her.

"Hadn't you better be going and looking what has become of Margery?" asked the Vicar in tones of reprimand.

"She is with her mother—I heared her. I will go in a whai-ile," smiled the girl coolly.

"Do you feel as if you could stand?" asked the father, still anxiously.

"Aye, in a bit," smiled Maurice.

"You want to get up?" caressed the girl, bowing over him, till her face was not far from his.

"I'm in no hurry," he replied, smiling brilliantly.

This accident had given him quite a strange new ease, an authority. He felt extraordinarily glad. New power had come to him all at once.

"You in no hurry," she repeated, gathering his meaning. She smiled tenderly: she was in his service.

"She leaves us in another month—Mrs. Inwood could stand no more of her," apologised the Vicar quietly to the father.

"Why, is she——"

"Like a wild thing—disobedient and insolent."

"Ha!"

The father sounded abstract.

"No more foreign governesses for me."

Maurice stirred, and looked up at the girl.

"You stand up?" she asked brightly. "You well?"

He laughed again, showing his teeth winsomely. She lifted his head, sprang to her feet, her hands still holding his head, then she took him under the armpits and had him on his feet before anyone could help. He was much taller than she. He grasped her strong shoulders heavily, leaned against her, and, feeling her round, firm breast doubled up against his side, he smiled, catching his breath.

"You see, I'm all right," he gasped. "I was only winded."

"You all raïght?" she cried, in great glee.

"Yes, I am."

He walked a few steps after a moment.

"There's nowt ails me, father," he laughed.

"Quite well, you?" she cried in a pleading tone. He laughed outright, looked down at her, touching her cheek with his fingers.

"That's it—if tha likes."

"If I lai-ike!" she repeated, radiant.

"She's going at the end of three weeks," said the Vicar consolingly to the farmer.

While they were talking, they heard the far-off hooting of a pit.

"There goes th' loose 'a," said Henry coldly. "We're *not* going to get that corner up to-day."

The father looked round anxiously.

"Now, Maurice, are you sure you're all right?" he asked.

"Yes, I'm all right. Haven't I told you?"

"Then you sit down there, and in a bit you can be getting dinner out. Henry, you go on the stack. Wheer's Jim? Oh, he's minding the hosses. Bill, and you, Geoffrey, you can pick while Jim loads."

Maurice sat down under the wych elm to recover. The Fräulein had fled back. He made up his mind to ask her to marry him. He had got fifty pounds of his own, and his mother would help him. For a long time he sat musing, thinking what he would do. Then, from the float he fetched a big basket covered with a cloth, and spread the dinner. There was an immense rabbit-pie, a dish of cold potatoes, much bread, a great piece of cheese, and a solid rice pudding.

20   These two fields were four miles from the home farm.

But they had been in the hands of the Wookeys for several generations, therefore the father kept them on, and everyone looked forward to the hay harvest at Greasley: it was a kind of picnic. They brought dinner and tea in the milk-float, which the father drove over in the morning. The lads and the labourers cycled. Off and on, the harvest lasted a fortnight. As the high road from Alfreton to Nottingham ran at the foot of the fields, someone usually slept in the hay under the shed to guard the tools. The sons took it in turns. They did not care for it much, and were for that reason anxious to finish the harvest on this day. But work went slack and disjointed after Maurice's accident.

When the load was teemed, they gathered round the white cloth, which was spread under a tree between the hedge and the stack, and, sitting on the ground, ate their meal. Mrs. Wookey sent always a clean cloth, and knives and forks and plates for everybody. Mr. Wookey was always rather proud of this spread: everything was so proper.

"There now," he said, sitting down jovially. "Doesn't this look nice now—eh?"

They all sat round the white spread, in the shadow of the tree and the stack, and looked out up the fields as they ate. From their shady coolness, the gold sward seemed liquid, molten with heat. The horse with the empty wagon wandered a few yards, then stood feeding. Everything was still as a trance. Now and again, the horse between the shafts of the load that stood propped beside the stack, jingled his loose bit as he ate. The men ate and drank in silence, the father reading the newspaper, Maurice leaning back on a saddle, Henry reading the *Nation*, the others eating busily.

Presently "Helloa! 'Er's 'ere again!" exclaimed Bill. All looked up. Paula was coming across the field carrying a plate.

"She's bringing something to tempt your appetite, Maurice," said the eldest brother ironically. Maurice was midway through a large wedge of rabbit-pie and some cold potatoes.

"Aye, bless me if she's not," laughed the father. "Put that away, Maurice, it's a shame to disappoint her."

Maurice looked round very shamefaced, not knowing what to do with his plate.

"Give it over here," said Bill. "I'll polish him off."

"Bringing something for the invalid?" laughed the father to the Fräulein. "He's looking up nicely."

"I bring him some chicken, him!" She nodded her head at Maurice childishly. He flushed and smiled.

"Tha doesna mean ter bust 'im," said Bill.

Everybody laughed aloud. The girl did not understand, so she laughed also. Maurice ate his portion very sheepishly.

The father pitied his son's shyness.

"Come here and sit by me," he said. "Eh, Fräulein! is that what they call you?"

"I sit by you, father," she said innocently.

Henry threw his head back and laughed long and noiselessly.

She settled near to the big, handsome man.

"My name," she said, "is Paula Jablonowsky."

"Is what?" said the father, and the other men went into roars of laughter.

"Tell me again," said the father. "Your name——"

"Paula."

"Paula? Oh—well, it's a rum sort of name, eh? His name——" he nodded at his son.

"Maurice—I know." She pronounced it sweetly, then laughed into the father's eyes. Maurice blushed to the roots of his hair.

They questioned her concerning her history, and made out that she came from Hanover, that her father was a shopkeeper, and that she had run away from home because she did not like her father. She had gone to Paris.

"Oh," said the father, now dubious. "And what did you do there?"

"In school—in a young ladies' school."

"Did you like it?"

"Oh no—no laïfe—no life!"

"What?"

"When we go out—two and two—all together—no more. Ah, no life, no life."

"Well, that's a winder!" exclaimed the father. "No life in Paris! And have you found much life in England?"

"No—ah no. I don't like it." She made a grimace at the Vicarage.

"How long have you been in England?"

"Chreestmas—so."

"And what will you do?"

"I will go to London, or to Paris. Ah, Paris!—Or get married!" She laughed into the father's eyes.

The father laughed heartily.

"Get married, eh? And who to?"

"I don't know. I am going away."

"The country's too quiet for you?" asked the father.

"Too quiet—hm!" she nodded in assent.

"You wouldn't care for making butter and cheese?"

"Making butter—hm!" She turned to him with a glad, bright gesture. "I like it."

"Oh," laughed the father. "You would, would you?"

She nodded vehemently, with glowing eyes.

"She'd like anything in the shape of a change," said Henry judicially.

"I think she would," agreed the father. It did not occur to them that she fully understood what they said. She looked at them closely, then thought with bowed head.

24   "Hullo!" exclaimed Henry, the alert. A tramp was

slouching towards them through the gap. He was a very seedy, slinking fellow, with a tang of horsey braggadocio about him. Small, thin, and ferrety, with a week's red beard bristling on his pointed chin, he came slouching forward.

"Have yer got a bit of a job goin'?" he asked.

"A bit of a job," repeated the father. "Why, can't you see as we've a'most done?"

"Aye—but I noticed you was a hand short, an' I thowt as 'appen you'd gie me half a day."

"What, are *you* any good in a hay close?" asked Henry, with a sneer.

The man stood slouching against the haystack. All the others were seated on the floor. He had an advantage.

"I could work aside any on yer," he bragged.

"Tha looks it," laughed Bill.

"And what's your regular trade?" asked the father.

"I'm a jockey by rights. But I did a bit o' dirty work for a boss o' mine, an' I was landed. *'E* got the benefit, *I* got kicked out. *'E* axed me—an' then 'e looked as if 'e'd never seed me."

"Did he, though!" exclaimed the father sympathetically.

" 'E did that!" asserted the man.

"But we've got nothing for you," said Henry coldly.

"What does the boss say?" asked the man, impudent.

"No, we've no work you can do," said the father. "You can have a bit o' something to eat, if you like."

"I should be glad of it," said the man. 25

He was given the chunk of rabbit-pie that remained. This he ate greedily. There was something debased, parasitic, about him, which disgusted Henry. The others regarded him as a curiosity.

"That was nice and tasty," said the tramp, with gusto.

"Do you want a piece of bread 'n' cheese?" asked the father.

"It'll help to fill up," was the reply.

The man ate this more slowly. The company was embarrassed by his presence, and could not talk. All the men lit their pipes, the meal over.

"So you dunna want any help?" said the tramp at last.

"No—we can manage what bit there is to do."

"You don't happen to have a fill of bacca to spare, do you?"

The father gave him a good pinch.

"You're all right here," he said, looking round. They resented this familiarity. However, he filled his clay pipe and smoked with the rest.

As they were sitting silent, another figure came through the gap in the hedge, and noiselessly approached. It was a woman. She was rather small and finely made. Her face was small, very ruddy, and comely, save for the look of bitterness and aloofness that it wore. Her hair was drawn tightly back under a sailor hat. She gave an impression of
cleanness, of precision and directness.

"Have you got some work?" she asked of her man. She ignored the rest. He tucked his tail between his legs.

"No, they haven't got no work for me. They've just gave me a draw of bacca."

He was a mean crawl of a man.

"An' am I goin' to wait for you out there on the lane all day?"

"You needn't if you don't like. You could go on."

"Well, are you coming?" she asked contemptuously. He rose to his feet in a rickety fashion.

"You needn't be in such a mighty hurry," he said. "If you'd wait a bit you might get summat."

She glanced for the first time over the men. She was quite young, and would have been pretty, were she not so hard and callous-looking.

"Have you had your dinner?" asked the father.

She looked at him with a kind of anger and turned away. Her face was so childish in its contours, contrasting strangely with her expression.

"Are you coming?" she said to the man.

"He's had his tuck-in. Have a bit, if you want it," coaxed the father.

"What have you had?" she flashed to the man.

"He's had all what was left o' th' rabbit-pie," said Geoffrey, in an indignant, mocking tone, "and a great hunk o' bread an' cheese."

"Well, it was gave me," said the man.

The young woman looked at Geoffrey, and he at her. There was a sort of kinship between them. Both were at odds with the world. Geoffrey smiled satirically. She was too grave, too deeply incensed even to smile.

"There's a cake here, though—you can have a bit o' that," said Maurice blithely.

She eyed him with scorn.

Again she looked at Geoffrey. He seemed to understand her. She turned, and in silence departed. The man remained obstinately sucking at his pipe. Everybody looked at him with hostility.

"We'll be getting to work," said Henry, rising, pulling off his coat. Paula got to her feet. She was a little bit confused by the presence of the tramp.

"I go," she said, smiling brilliantly. Maurice rose and followed her sheepishly.

"A good grind, eh?" said the tramp, nodding after the Fräulein. The men only half understood him, but they hated him.

"Hadn't you better be getting off?" said Henry.

The man rose obediently. He was all slouching, parasitic insolence. Geoffrey loathed him, longed to exterminate him. He was exactly the worst foe of the hypersensitive: insolence without sensibility, preying on sensibility.

"Aren't you goin' to give me summat for her? It's nowt she's had all day, to my knowin'. She'll 'appen eat it if I take it 'er—though she gets more than I've any knowledge of"—this with a lewd wink of jealous spite. "And then tries to keep a tight hand on me," he sneered, taking the bread and cheese, and stuffing it in his pocket.

3

Geoffrey worked sullenly all the afternoon, and Maurice did the horse-raking. It was exceedingly hot. So the day wore on, the atmosphere thickened, and the sunlight grew blurred. Geoffrey was picking with Bill—helping to load the wagons from the winrows. He was sulky, though extraordinarily relieved: Maurice would not tell. Since the quarrel neither brother had spoken to the other. But their silence was entirely amicable, almost affectionate. They had both been deeply moved, so much so that their ordinary intercourse was interrupted: but underneath, each felt a strong regard for the other. Maurice was peculiarly happy, his feeling of affection swimming over everything. But Geoffrey was still sullenly hostile to the most part of the world. He felt isolated. The free and easy intercommunication between the other workers left him distinctly alone. And he was a man who could not bear to stand alone, he was too much afraid of the vast confusion of life surrounding him, in which he was helpless. Geoffrey mistrusted himself with everybody.

The work went on slowly. It was unbearably hot, and everyone was disheartened.

"We s'll have getting-on-for another day of it," said the father at tea-time, as they sat under the tree.

"Quite a day," said Henry.

"Somebody'll have to stop, then," said Geoffrey. "It 'ud better be me."

"Nay, lad, I'll stop," said Maurice, and he hid his head in confusion.

"Stop again to-night!" exclaimed the father. "I'd rather you went home."

"Nay, I'm stoppin'," protested Maurice.

"He wants to do his courting," Henry enlightened them.

The father thought seriously about it.

"I don't know . . . ," he mused, rather perturbed.

But Maurice stayed. Towards eight o'clock, after sundown, the man mounted their bicycles, the father put the horse in the float, and all departed. Maurice stood in the gap of the hedge and watched them go, the cart rolling and swinging down-hill, over the grass stubble, the cyclists dipping swiftly like shadows in front. All passed through the gate, there was a quick clatter of hoofs on the roadway under the lime trees, and they were gone. The young man was very much excited, almost afraid, at finding himself alone.

Darkness was rising from the valley. Already, up the steep hill the cart-lamps crept indecisively, and the cottage windows were lit. Everything looked strange to Maurice, as if he had not seen it before. Down the hedge a large lime tree teemed with scent that seemed almost like a voice speaking. It startled him. He caught a breath of the over-sweet fragrance, then stood still, listening expectantly.

Up-hill, a horse whinneyed. It was the young mare. The heavy horses went thundering across to the far hedge.

Maurice wondered what to do. He wandered round the deserted stacks restlessly. Heat came in wafts, in thick strands. The evening was a long time cooling. He thought he would go and wash himself. There was a trough of pure water in the hedge bottom. It was filled by a tiny spring that filtered over the brim of the trough down the lush hedge bottom of the lower field. All round the trough, in the upper field, the land was marshy, and there the meadow-sweet stood like clots of mist, very sickly-smelling in the twilight. The night did not darken, for the moon was in the sky, so that as the tawny colour drew off the heavens they remained pallid with a dimmed moon. The purple bell-flowers in the hedge went black, the ragged robin turned its pink to a faded white, the meadow-sweet gathered light as if it were phosphorescent, and it made the air ache with scent.

Maurice kneeled on the slab of stone bathing his hands

and arms, then his face. The water was deliciously cool. He had still an hour before Paula would come: she was not due till nine. So he decided to take his bath at night instead of waiting till morning. Was he not sticky, and was not Paula coming to talk to him? He was delighted the thought had occurred to him. As he soused his head in the trough, he wondered what the little creatures that lived in the velvety silt at the bottom would think of the taste of soap. Laughing to himself, he squeezed his cloth into the water. He washed himself from head to foot, standing in the fresh, forsaken corner of the field, where no one could see him by daylight, so that now, in the veiled grey tinge of moonlight, he was no more noticeable than the crowded flowers. The night had on a new look: he never remembered to have seen the lustrous grey sheen of it before, nor to have noticed how vital the lights looked, like live folk inhabiting the silvery spaces. And the tall trees, wrapped obscurely in their mantles, would not have surprised him had they begun to move in converse. As he dried himself, he discovered little wanderings in the air, felt on his sides soft touches and caresses that were peculiarly delicious: sometimes they startled him, and he laughed as if he were not alone. The flowers, the meadow-sweet particularly, haunted him. He reached to put his hand over their fleeciness. They touched his thighs. Laughing, he gathered them and dusted himself all over with their cream dust and fragrance. For a moment he hesitated in wonder at himself: but the subtle glow in the hoary and black night reassured him. Things never had looked so personal and full of beauty, he had never known the wonder in himself before.

At nine o'clock he was waiting under the elder bush, in a state of high trepidation, but feeling that he was worthy, having a sense of his own wonder. She was late. At a quarter-past nine she came, flitting swiftly, in her own eager way.

"No, she would *not* go to sleep," said Paula, with a world of wrath in her tone. He laughed bashfully. They wandered out into the dim, hill-side field.

"I have sat—in that bedroom—for an hour, for hours," she cried indignantly. She took a deep breath: "Ah, breathe!" she smiled.

She was very intense, and full of energy.

"I want"—she was clumsy with the language—"I want—I should laike—to run—there!" She pointed across the field.

"Let's run, then," he said curiously.

"Yes!"

And in an instant she was gone. He raced after her. For all he was so young and limber, he had difficulty in catching her. At first he could scarcely see her, though he could hear the rustle of her dress. She sped with astonishing fleetness. He overtook her, caught her by the arm, and they stood panting, facing one another with laughter.

"I could win," she asserted blithely.

"Tha couldna," he replied, with a peculiar, excited laugh. They walked on, rather breathless. In front of them suddenly appeared the dark shapes of the three feeding horses.

"We ride a horse?" she said.

"What, bareback?" he asked.

"You say?" She did not understand.

"With no saddle?"

"No saddle—yes—no saddle."

"Coop, lass!" he said to the mare, and in a minute he had her by the forelock, and was leading her down to the stacks, where he put a halter on her. She was a big, strong mare. Maurice seated the Fräulein, clambered himself in front of the girl, using the wheel of the wagon as a mount, and together they trotted uphill, she holding lightly round his waist. From the crest of the hill they looked round.

The sky was darkening with an awning of cloud. On the left the hill rose black and wooded, made cosy by a few lights from cottages long the highway. The hill spread to the right, and tufts of trees shut round. But in front was a great vista of night, a sprinkle of cottage candles, a twinkling cluster of lights, like an elfish fair in full swing, at the colliery, an encampment of light at a village, a red flare on the sky far off, above an iron-foundry, and in the farthest distance the dim breathing of town lights. As they watched the night stretch far out, her arms tightened round his waist, and he pressed his elbows to his side, pressing her arms closer still. The horse moved restlessly. They clung to each other.

"Tha daesna want to go right away?" he asked the girl behind him.

"I stay with you," she answered softly, and he felt her crouching close against him. He laughed curiously. He was afraid to kiss her, though he was urged to do so. They remained still, on the restless horse, watching the small lights lead deep into the night, an infinite distance.

"I don't want to go," he said, in a tone half pleading. She did not answer. The horse stirred restlessly.

"Let him run," cried Paula, "fast!"

She broke the spell, startled him into a little fury. He kicked the mare, hit her, and away she plunged down-hill. The girl clung tightly to the young man. They were riding bareback down a rough, steep hill. Maurice clung hard with hands and knees. Paula held him fast round the waist, leaning her head on his shoulders, and thrilling with excitement.

"We shall be off, we shall be off," he cried, laughing with excitement; but she only crouched behind and pressed tight to him. The mare tore across the field. Maurice expected every moment to be flung on to the grass. He gripped with all the strength of his knees. Paula tucked herself behind him, and often wrenched him almost from his hold. Man and girl were taut with effort.

At last the mare came to a standstill, blowing. Paula slid

off, and in an instant Maurice was beside her. They were both highly excited. Before he knew what he was doing, he had her in his arms, fast, and was kissing her, and laughing. They did not move for some time. Then, in silence, they walked towards the stacks.

It had grown quite dark, the night was thick with cloud. He walked with his arm round Paula's waist, she with her arm round him. They were near the stacks when Maurice felt a spot of rain.

"It's going to rain," he said.

"Rain!" she echoed, as if it were trivial.

"I s'll have to put the stack-cloth on," he said gravely. She did not understand.

When they got to the stacks, he went round to the shed, to return staggering in the darkness under the burden of the immense and heavy cloth. It had not been used once during the hay harvest.

"What are you going to do?" asked Paula, coming close to him in the darkness.

"Cover the top of the stack with it," he replied. "Put it over the stack, to keep the rain out."

"Ah!" she cried, "up there!" He dropped his burden.

"Yes," he answered.

Fumblingly he reared the long ladder up the side of the stack. He could not see the top.

"I hope it's solid," he said softly.

A few smart drops of rain sounded drumming on the

cloth. They seemed like another presence. It was very dark indeed between the great buildings of hay. She looked up the black wall and shrank to him.

"You carry it up there?" she asked.

"Yes," he answered.

"I help you?" she said.

And she did. They opened the cloth. He clambered first up the steep ladder, bearing the upper part, she followed closely, carrying her full share. They mounted the shaky ladder in silence, stealthily.

4

As they climbed the stacks a light stopped at the gate on the high road. It was Geoffrey, come to help his brother with the cloth. Afraid of his own intrusion, he wheeled his bicycle silently towards the shed. This was a corrugated iron erection, on the opposite side of the hedge from the stacks. Geoffrey let his light go in front of him, but there was no sign from the lovers. He thought he saw a shadow slinking away. The light of the bicycle lamp sheered yellowly across the dark, catching a glint of raindrops, a mist of darkness, shadow of leaves and strokes of long grass. Geoffrey entered the shed—no one was there. 37

He walked slowly and doggedly round to the stacks. He had passed the wagon, when he heard something sheering down upon him. Starting back under the wall of hay, he saw the long ladder slither across the side of the stack, and fall with a bruising ring.

"What wor that?" he heard Maurice, aloft, ask cautiously.

"Something fall," came the curious, almost pleased voice of the Fräulein.

"It wor niver th' ladder," said Maurice. He peered over the side of the stack. He lay down, looking.

"It is an' a'!" he exclaimed. "We knocked it down with the cloth, dragging it over."

"We fast up here?" she exclaimed with a thrill.

"We are that—without I shout and make 'em hear at the Vicarage."

"Oh no," she said quickly.

"I don't want to," he replied, with a short laugh. There came a swift clatter of raindrops on the cloth. Geoffrey crouched under the wall of the other stack.

"Mind where you tread—here, let me straighten this end," said Maurice, with a peculiar intimate tone—a command and an embrace. "We s'll have to sit under it. At any rate, we shan't get wet."

"Not get wet!" echoed the girl, pleased, but agitated.

Geoffrey heard the slide and rustle of the cloth over

the top of the stack, heard Maurice telling her to "Mind!"

"Mind!" she repeated. "Mind! you say 'Mind!'"

"Well, what if I do?" he laughed. "I don't want you to fall over th' side, do I?" His tone was masterful, but he was not quite sure of himself.

There was silence a moment or two.

"Maurice!" she said plaintively.

"I'm here," he answered tenderly, his voice shaky with excitement that was near to distress. "There, I've done. Now should we—we'll sit under this corner."

"Maurice!" she said plaintively.

"What? You'll be all right," he remonstrated, tenderly indignant.

"I be all raïght," she repeated, "I be all raïght, Maurice?"

"Tha knows tha will—I canna ca' thee Powla. Should I ca' thee Minnie?"

It was the name of a dead sister.

"Minnie?" she exclaimed in surprise.

"Aye, should I?"

She answered in full-throated German. He laughed shakily.

"Come on—come on under. But do yer wish you was safe in th' Vicarage? Should I shout for somebody?" he asked.

"I don't wish, no!" She was vehement.

"Art sure?" he insisted, almost indignantly.

"Sure—I quite sure." She laughed.

39

Geoffrey turned away at the last words. Then the rain beat heavily. The lonely brother slouched miserably to the hut, where the rain played a mad tattoo. He felt very miserable, and jealous of Maurice.

His bicycle lamp, downcast, shone a yellow light on the stark floor of the shed or hut with one wall open. It lit up the trodden earth, the shafts of tools lying piled under the beam, beside the dreary grey metal of the building. He took off the lamp, shone it round the hut. There were piles of harness, tools, a big sugar-box, a deep bed of hay—then the beams across the corrugated iron, all very dreary and stark. He shone the lamp into the night: nothing but the furtive glitter of raindrops through the mist of darkness, and black shapes hovering round.

Geoffrey blew out the light and flung himself on to the hay. He would put the ladder up for them in a while, when they would be wanting it. Meanwhile he sat and gloated over Maurice's felicity. He was imaginative, and now he had something concrete to work upon. Nothing in the whole of life stirred him so profoundly, and so utterly, as the thought of this woman. For Paula was strange, foreign, different from the ordinary girls: the rousing, feminine quality seemed in her concentrated, brighter, more fascinating than in anyone he had known, so that he felt most like a moth near a candle. He would have loved her wildly—but Maurice had got her. His thoughts beat the same course, round and round. What was it like when you kissed her, when she held you tight round the waist, how did she feel towards Maurice, did she love to touch him, was he fine and attractive to her; what did she think of himself—she merely disregarded him, as she would disregard a horse in a field; why would she do so, why couldn't he make her regard himself, instead of Maurice: he would never command a woman's regard like that, he always gave in to her too soon; if only some woman would come and take him for what he was worth, though he was such a stumbler and showed to such disadvantage, ah, what a grand thing it would be; how he would kiss her. Then round he went again in the same course, brooding almost like a madman. Meanwhile the rain drummed deep on the shed, then grew lighter and softer. There came the drip, drip of the drops falling outside.

Geoffrey's heart leaped up his chest, and he clenched himself, as a black shape crept round the post of the shed and, bowing, entered silently. The young man's heart beat so heavily in plunges, he could not get his breath to speak. It was shock, rather than fear. The form felt towards him. He sprang up, gripped it with his great hands panting "Now, then!"

There was no resistance, only a little whimper of despair.

"Let me go," said a woman's voice.

"What are you after?" he asked, in deep, gruff tones.

"I thought 'e was 'ere," she wept despairingly, with little, stubborn sobs.

"An' you've found what you didn't expect, have you?"

At the sound of his bullying she tried to get away from him.

"Let me go," she said.

"Who did you expect to find here?" he asked, but more his natural self.

"I expected my husband—him as you saw at dinner. Let me go."

"Why, is it you?" exclaimed Geoffrey. "Has he left you?"

"Let me go," said the woman sullenly, trying to draw away. He realised that her sleeve was very wet, her arm slender under his grasp. Suddenly he grew ashamed of himself: he had no doubt hurt her, gripping her so hard. He relaxed, but did not let her go.

"An' are you searching round after that snipe as was here at dinner?" he asked. She did not answer.

"Where did he leave you?"

"I left him—here. I've seen nothing of him since."

"I s'd think it's good riddance," he said. She did not answer. He gave a short laugh, saying:

"I should ha' thought you wouldn't ha' wanted to clap eyes on him again."

"He's my husband—an' he's not goin' to run off if I can stop him."

Geoffrey was silent, not knowing what to say.

"Have you got a jacket on?" he asked at last.

"What do you think? You've got hold of it."

"You're wet through, aren't you?"

"I shouldn't be dry, comin' through that teemin' rain. But 'e's not here, so I'll go."

"I mean," he said humbly, "are you wet through?"

She did not answer. He felt her shiver.

"Are you cold?" he asked, in surprise and concern.

She did not answer. He did not know what to say.

"Stop a minute," he said, and he fumbled in his pocket for his matches. He struck a light, holding it in the hollow of his large, hard palm. He was a big man, and he looked anxious. Shedding the light on her, he saw she was rather pale, and very weary looking. Her old sailor hat was sodden and drooping with rain. She wore a fawn-coloured jacket of smooth cloth. This jacket was black-wet where the rain had beaten, her skirt hung sodden, and dripped on to her boots. The match went out.

"Why, you're wet through!" he said.

She did not answer.

"Shall you stop in here while it gives over?" he asked.

She did not answer.

" 'Cause if you will, you'd better take your things off, an' have th' rug. There's a horse-rug in the box."

He waited, but she would not answer. So he lit his bicycle lamp, and rummaged in the box, pulling out a large brown blanket, striped with scarlet and yellow. She stood stock still. He shone the light on her. She was very pale, and trembling fitfully.

"Are you that cold?" he asked in concern. "Take your jacket off, and your hat, and put this right over you."

Mechanically, she undid the enormous fawn-coloured buttons, and unpinned her hat. With her black hair drawn back from her low, honest brow, she looked little more than a girl, like a girl driven hard with womanhood by stress of life. She was small, and natty, with neat little features. But she shivered convulsively.

"Is something a-matter with you?" he asked.

"I've walked to Bulwell and back," she quivered, "looking for him—an' I've not touched a thing since this morning." She did not weep—she was too dreary-hardened to cry. He looked at her in dismay, his mouth half open: "Gormin" as Maurice would have said.

" 'Aven't you had nothing to eat?" he said.

Then he turned aside to the box. There, the bread remaining was kept, and the great piece of cheese, and such things as sugar and salt, with all table utensils; there was some butter.

She sat down drearily on the bed of hay. He cut her a piece of bread and butter, and a piece of cheese. This she took, but ate listlessly.

"I want a drink," she said.

"We 'aven't got no beer," he answered. "My father doesn't have it."

"I want water,' she said.

He took a can and plunged through the wet darkness,

under the great black hedge, down to the trough. As he came back he saw her in the half-lit little cave sitting bunched together. The soaked grass wet his feet—he thought of her. When he gave her a cup of water, her hand touched his and he felt her fingers hot and glossy. She trembled so she spilled the water.

"Do you feel badly?" he asked.

"I can't keep myself still—but it's only with being tired and having nothing to eat."

He scratched his head contemplatively, waited while she ate her piece of bread and butter. Then he offered her another piece.

"I don't want it just now," she said.

"You'll have to eat summat," he said.

"I couldn't eat any more just now."

He put the piece down undecidedly on the box. Then there was another long pause. He stood up with bent head. The bicycle, like a restful animal, flittered behind him, turning towards the wall. The woman sat hunched on the hay, shivering.

"Can't you get warm?" he asked.

"I shall by an' by—don't you bother. I'm taking your seat—are you stopping here all night?"

"Yes."

"I'll be goin' in a bit," she said.

"Nay, I non want you to go. I'm thinkin' how you could get warm."

"Don't you bother about me," she remonstrated, almost irritably.

"I just want to see as the stacks is all right. You take your shoes an' stockin's an' all your wet things off: you can easy wrap yourself all over in that rug, there's not so much of you."

"It's raining—I s'll be all right—I s'll be going in a minute."

"I've got to see as the stacks is safe. Take your wet things off."

"Are you coming back?" she asked.

"I mightn't, not till morning."

"Well, I s'll be gone in ten minutes, then. I've no rights to be here, an' I s'll not let anybody be turned out for me."

"You won't be turning me out."

"Whether or no, I shan't stop."

"Well, shall you if I come back?" he asked. She did not answer.

He went. In a few moments, she blew the light out. The rain was falling steadily, and the night was a black gulf. All was intensely still. Geoffrey listened everywhere: no sound save the rain. He stood between the stacks, but only heard the trickle of water, and the light swish of rain. Everything was lost in blackness. He imagined death was like that, many things dissolved in silence and darkness, blotted out, but existing. In the dense blackness he felt himself almost extinguished. He was afraid he might not

46

find things the same. Almost frantically, he stumbled, feeling his way, till his hand touched the wet metal. He had been looking for a gleam of light.

"Did you blow the lamp out?" he asked, fearful lest the silence should answer him.

"Yes," she answered humbly. He was glad to hear her voice. Groping into the pitch-dark shed, he knocked against the box, part of whose cover served as table. There was a clatter and a fall.

"That's the lamp, an' the knife, an' the cup," he said. He struck a match.

"Th' cup's not broke." He put it into the box.

"But th' oil's spilled out o' th' lamp. It always was a rotten old thing.' He hastily blew out his match, which was burning his fingers. Then he struck another light.

"You don't want a lamp, you know you don't, and I s'll be going directly, so you come an' lie down an' get your night's rest. I'm not taking any of your place."

He looked at her by the light of another match. She was a queer little bundle, all brown, with gaudy border folding in and out, and her little face peering at him. As the match went out she saw him beginning to smile.

"I can sit right at this end," she said. "You lie down."

He came and sat on the hay, at some distance from her. After a spell of silence:

"Is he really your husband?" he asked.

"He is!" she answered grimly.

"Hm!" Then there was silence again.

After a while: "Are you warm now?"

"Why do you bother yourself?"

"I don't bother myself—do you follow him because you like him?" He put it very timidly. He wanted to know.

"I don't—I wish he was dead," this with bitter contempt. Then doggedly: "But he's my husband."

He gave a short laugh.

"By Gad!" he said.

Again, after a while: "Have you been married long?"

"Four years."

"Four years—why, how old are you?"

"Twenty-three."

"Are you turned twenty-three?"

"Last May."

"Then you're four month older than me." He mused over it. They were only two voices in the pitch-black night. It was eerie silence again.

"And do you just tramp about?" he asked.

"He reckons he's looking for a job. But he doesn't like work in any shape or form. He was a stableman when I married him, at Greenhalgh's, the horse-dealers, at Chesterfield, where I was housemaid. He left that job when the baby was only two months, and I've been badgered about from pillar to post ever sin'. They say a rolling stone gathers no moss. . . ."

"An' where's the baby?"

"It died when it was ten months old."

Now the silence was clinched between them. It was quite a long time before Geoffrey ventured to say sympathetically: "You haven't much to look forward to."

"I've wished many a score time when I've started shiverin' an' shakin' at nights, as I was taken bad for death. But we're not that handy at dying."

He was silent. "But whatever shall you do?" he faltered.

"I s'll find him, if I drop by th' road."

"Why?" he asked, wondering, looking her way, though he saw nothing but solid darkness.

"Because I shall. He's not going to have it all his own road."

"But why don't you leave him?"

"Because he's *not goin' to have it all his own road.*"

She sounded very determined, even vindictive. He sat in wonder, feeling uneasy, and vaguely miserable on her behalf. She sat extraordinarily still. She seemed like a voice only, a presence.

"Are you warm now?" he asked, half afraid.

"A bit warmer—but my feet!" She sounded pitiful.

"Let me warm them with my hands," he asked her. "I'm hot enough."

"No, thank you," she said coldly.

Then, in the darkness, she felt she had wounded him. He was writhing under her rebuff, for his offer had been pure kindness.

49

"They're 'appen dirty," she said, half mocking.

"Well—mine is—an' I have a bath a'most every day," he answered.

"I don't know when they'll get warm," she moaned to herself.

"Well, then, put them in my hands."

She heard him faintly rattling the match-box, and then a phosphorescent glare began to fume in his direction. Presently he was holding two smoking, blue-green blotches of light towards her feet. She was afraid. But her feet ached so, and the impulse drove her on, so she placed her soles lightly on the two blotches of smoke. His large hands clasped over her instep, warm and hard.

"They're like ice!" he said, in deep concern.

He warmed her feet as best he could, putting them close against him. Now and again convulsive tremors ran over her. She felt his warm breath on the balls of her toes, that were bunched up in his hands. Leaning forward, she touched his hair delicately with her fingers. He thrilled. She fell to gently stroking his hair, with timid, pleading finger-tips.

"Do they feel any better?" he asked, in a low voice, suddenly lifting his face to her. This sent her hand sliding softly over his face, and her finger-tips caught on his mouth. She drew quickly away. He put his hand out to find hers, in his other palm holding both her feet. His 50 wandering hand met her face. He touched it curiously. It was wet. He put his big fingers cautiously on her eyes, into two little pools of tears.

"What's a matter?" he asked in a low, choked voice.

She leaned down to him and gripped him tightly round the neck, pressing him to her bosom in a little frenzy of pain. Her bitter disillusionment with life, her unalleviated shame and degradation during the last four years, had driven her into loneliness, and hardened her till a large part of her nature was caked and sterile. Now she softened again, and her spring might be beautiful. She had been in a fair way to make an ugly old woman.

She clasped the head of Geoffrey to her breast, which heaved and fell, and heaved again. He was bewildered, full of wonder. He allowed the woman to do as she would with him. Her tears fell on his hair, as she wept noiselessly; and he breathed deep as she did. At last she let go her clasp. He put his arms round her.

"Come and let me warm you," he said, folding up on his knee and lapping her with his heavy arms against himself. She was small and *câline*. He held her very warm and close. Presently she stole her arms round him.

"You *are* big," she whispered.

He gripped her hard, started, put his mouth down wanderingly, seeking her out. His lips met her temple. She slowly, deliberately turned her mouth to his, and with opened lips, met him in a kiss, his first love kiss.

5

It was breaking cold dawn when Geoffrey woke. The woman was still sleeping in his arms. Her face in sleep moved all his tenderness: the tight shutting of her mouth, as if in resolution to bear what was very hard to bear, contrasted so pitifully with the small mould of her features. Geoffrey pressed her to his bosom: having her, he felt he could bruise the lips of the scornful, and pass on erect, unabateable. With her to complete him, to form the core of him, he was firm and whole. Needing her so much, he loved her fervently.

Meanwhile the dawn came like death, one of those slow, livid mornings that seem to come in a cold sweat. Slowly, and painfully, the air began to whiten. Geoffrey saw it was not raining. As he was watching the ghastly transformation outside, he felt aware of something. He glanced down: she was open-eyed, watching him; she had golden-brown, calm eyes, that immediately smiled into his. He also smiled, bowed softly down and kissed her. They did not speak for some time. Then:

"What's thy name?" he asked curiously.

"Lydia," she said.

"Lydia!" he repeated wonderingly. He felt rather shy.

"Mine's Geoffrey Wookey," he said.

She merely smiled at him.

They were silent for a considerate time. By morning light, things look small. The huge trees of the evening were dwindled to hoary, small, uncertain things, trespassing in the sick pallor of the atmosphere. There was a dense mist, so that the light could scarcely breathe. Everything seemed to quiver with cold and sickliness.

"Have you often slept out?" he asked her.

"Not so very," she answered.

"You won't go after *him?*" he asked.

"I s'll have to," she replied, but she nestled in to Geoffrey. He felt a sudden panic.

"You mustn't," he exclaimed, and she saw he was afraid for himself. She let it be, was silent.

"We couldn't get married?" he asked thoughtfully.

"No."

He brooded deeply over this. At length:

"Would you go to Canada with me?"

"We'll see what you think in two months' time," she replied quietly, without bitterness.

"I s'll think the same," he protested, hurt.

She did not answer, only watched him steadily. She was there for him to do as he liked with; but she would not injure his fortunes; no, not to save his soul.

"Haven't you got no relations?" he asked.

"A married sister at Crick."

"On a farm?"

"No—married a farm labourer—but she's very comfortable. I'll go there, if you want me to, just till I can get another place in service."

He considered this.

"Could you get on a farm?" he asked wistfully.

"Greenhalgh's was a farm."

He saw the future brighten: she would be a help to him. She agreed to go to her sister, and to get a place of service—until spring, he said, when they would sail for Canada. He waited for her assent.

"You will come with me, then?" he asked.

"When the time comes," she said.

Her want of faith made him bow his head: she had reason for it.

"Shall you walk to Crick, or go from Langley Mill to Ambergate? But it's only ten mile to walk. So we can go together up Hunt's Hill—you'd have to go past our lane-end, then I could easy nip down an' fetch you some money," he said humbly.

"I've got half a sovereign by me—it's more than I s'll want."

"Let's see it," he said.

After a while, fumbling under the blanket, she brought
out the piece of money. He felt she was independent of

him. Brooding rather bitterly, he told himself she'd for-
sake him. His anger gave him courage to ask:

"Shall you go in service in your maiden name?"

"No."

He was bitterly wrathful with her—full of resentment.

"I bet I s'll niver see you again," he said, with a short,
hard laugh. She put her arms round him, pressed him to
her bosom, while the tears rose to her eyes. He was reassured, but not satisfied.

"Shall you write to me to-night?"

"Yes, I will."

"And can I write to you—who shall I write to?"

"Mrs. Bredon."

" 'Bredon'!" he repeated bitterly.

He was exceedingly uneasy.

The dawn had grown quite wan. He saw the hedges
drooping wet down the grey mist. Then he told her about
Maurice.

"Oh, you *shouldn't!*" she said. "You should ha' put the
ladder up for them, you *should.*"

"Well—I don't care."

"Go and do it now—and I'll go."

"No, don't you. Stop an' see our Maurice: go on, stop
an' see him—then I'll be able to tell him."

She consented in silence. He had her promise she would
not go before he returned. She adjusted her dress, found
her way to the trough, where she performed her toilet.

Geoffrey wandered round to the upper field. The stacks looked wet in the mist, the hedge was drenched. Mist rose like steam from the grass, and the near hills were veiled almost to a shadow. In the valley, some peaks of black poplar showed fairly definite, jutting up. He shivered with chill.

There was no sound from the stacks, and he could see nothing. After all, he wondered, were they up there? But he reared the ladder to the place whence it had been swept, then went down the hedge to gather dry sticks. He was breaking off thin dead twigs under a holly tree when he heard, on the perfectly still air: "Well, I'm dashed!"

He listened intently, Maurice was awake.

"Sithee here!" the lad's voice exclaimed. Then, after a while, the foreign sound of the girl:

"What—oh, thair!"

"Aye, th' ladder's there, right enough."

"You said it had fall down."

"Well, I heard it drop—an' I couldna feel it nor see it."

"You said it had fall down—you lie, you liar."

"Nay, as true as I'm here——"

"You tell me lies—make me stay here—you tell me lies——" She was passionately indignant.

"As true as I'm standing here——" he began.

"Lies!—lies!—lies!" she cried. "I don't believe you, never. You *mean*, you *mean*, *mean*, *mean!*"

"A' raïght, then!" He was now incensed, in his turn.

"You are bad, mean, mean, mean."

"Are ter commin' down?" asked Maurice coldly.

"No—I will not come with you—mean, to tell me lies."

"Are ter commin' down?"

"No, I don't want you."

"A' raïght, then!"

Geoffrey, peering through the holly tree, saw Maurice negotiating the ladder. The top rung was below the brim of the stack, and rested on the cloth, so it was dangerous to approach. The Fräulein watched him from the end of the stack, where the cloth thrown back showed the light, dry hay. He slipped slightly, she screamed. When he had got on to the ladder, he pulled the cloth away, throwing it back, making it easy for her to descend.

"Now are ter commin'?" he asked.

"No!" She shook her head violently, in a pet.

Geoffrey felt slightly contemptuous of her. But Maurice waited.

"Are ter commin'?" he called again.

"No," she flashed, like a wild cat.

"All right, then I'm going."

He descended. At the bottom, he stood holding the ladder.

"Come on, while I hold it steady," he said.

There was no reply. For some minutes he stood patiently with his foot on the bottom rung of the ladder. He was pale, rather washed-out in his appearance, and he drew himself together with cold.

"Are ter commin', or aren't ter?" he asked at length. Still there was no reply.

"Then stop up till tha'rt ready," he muttered, and he went away. Round the other side of the stacks he met Geoffrey.

"What, are thaïgh here?" he exclaimed.

"Bin here a' naïght," replied Geoffrey. "I come to help thee wi' th' cloth, but I found it on, an' th' ladder down, so I thowt tha'd gone."

"Did ter put th' ladder up?"

"I did a bit sin'."

Maurice brooded over this, Geoffrey struggled with himself to get out his own news. At last he blurted:

"Tha knows that woman as wor here yis'day dinner—'er come back, an' stopped i' th' shed a' night, out o' th' rain."

"Oh—ah!" said Maurice, his eye kindling, and a smile crossing his pallor.

"An' I s'll gi'e her some breakfast."

"Oh—ah!" repeated Maurice.

"It's th' man as is good-for-nowt, not her," protested Geoffrey. Maurice did not feel in a position to cast stones.

"Tha pleases thysen," he said, "what ter does." He was very quiet, unlike himself. He seemed bothered and anxious, as Geoffrey had not seen him before.

58

"What's up wi' thee?" asked the elder brother, who in his own heart was glad, and relieved.

"Nowt," was the reply.

They went together to the hut. The woman was folding the blanket. She was fresh from washing, and looked very pretty. Her hair, instead of being screwed tightly back, was coiled in a knot low down, partly covering her ears. Before she had deliberately made herself plain-looking: now she was neat and pretty, with a sweet, womanly gravity.

"Hello. I didn't think to find you here," said Maurice, very awkwardly, smiling. She watched him gravely without reply. "But it was better in shelter than outside last night," he added.

"Yes," she replied.

"Shall you get a few more sticks?" Geoffrey asked him. It was a new thing for Geoffrey to be leader. Maurice obeyed. He wandered forth into the damp, raw morning. He did not go to the stack, as he shrank from meeting Paula.

At the mouth of the hut, Geoffrey was making the fire. The woman got out coffee from the box: Geoffrey set the tin to boil. They were arranging breakfast when Paula appeared. She was hatless. Bits of hay stuck in her hair, and she was white-faced—altogether, she did not show to advantage.

"Ah—you!" she exclaimed, seeing Geoffrey.

"Hello!" he answered. "You're out early."

"Where's Maurice?"

"I dunno, he should be back directly."

Paula was silent.

"When have you come?" she asked.

"I come last night, but I could see nobody about. I got up half an hour sin', an' put th' ladder up ready to take the stack cloth up."

Paula understood, and was silent. When Maurice returned with the faggots, she was crouched warming her hands. She looked up at him, but he kept his eyes averted from her. Geoffrey met the eyes of Lydia, and smiled. Maurice put his hands to the fire.

"You cold?" asked Paula tenderly.

"A bit," he answered, quite friendly, but reserved. And all the while the four sat round the fire, drinking their smoked coffee, eating each a small piece of toasted bacon, Paula watched eagerly for the eyes of Maurice, and he avoided her. He was gentle, but would not give his eyes to her looks. And Geoffrey smiled constantly to Lydia, who watched gravely.

The German girl succeeded in getting safely into the Vicarage, her escapade unknown to anyone save the housemaid. Before a week was out, she was openly engaged to Maurice, and when her month's notice expired, she went to live at the farm.

Geoffrey and Lydia kept faith one with the other.